Stay Safe, Stay Smart

Your Safety Handbook

Priyanka Verma

DIAMOND BOOKS

www.diamondbooks.in

Publisher : **Diamond Pocket Books (P) Ltd.**
X-30, Okhla Industrial Area, Phase-II
New Delhi-110020
Phone : 011-40712200
E-mail : wecare@diamondbooks.in
Website : www.diamondbooks.in
Edition : 2025
Printed By : Repro (India)

Preface

Dear Readers,

Safety is something we all need—at home, on the road, online, and in public places. This book is designed just for you—to help you recognize what's safe, what's not, and how to respond wisely. Packed with fun stories, simple rules, real-life tips, and thoughtful activities, this book helps you become confident and smart in every situation.

Whether you're at school, playing outside, or chatting online, remember: Learning to stay safe is learning to live well!

Let's begin this safety adventure—together!

- Priyanka Verma

Foreword

"Children are curious explorers, and their safety begins with awareness. This book provides practical, age-appropriate tools that empower young minds to protect themselves and make wise choices. It supports NEP 2020's focus on life skills, emotional intelligence, and responsible citizenship. Every parent, teacher, and child will find immense value in its pages."

Contents

Chapter 1

Let's Begin Our Safety Journey!

Story: Meera's Day of Surprises

It was a bright Saturday morning. Meera, a cheerful and curious 10-year-old, was looking forward to the weekend. With no school and lots of playtime ahead, she had already made a plan with her cousin Kabir to build a cardboard rocket ship in the living room.
As Meera was cutting colored paper, the doorbell rang.
"I'll get it!" she said, running toward the door.

Through the peephole, she saw a man in a delivery uniform holding a brown box. "Delivery for Sharma house," he said.
Meera was about to unlock the door—but paused. Something her mother had said echoed in her head: "Don't open the door unless a grown-up says it's okay."

Instead of opening it, Meera ran to call her father. He came and collected the parcel safely. "Good job, Meera," he smiled. "That's how to stay safe."

Later that day, Meera and Kabir went out with their grandma to buy ice cream. On the way, they had to cross the street. Kabir rushed ahead. “Wait!” Meera called out. “Let’s cross at the zebra crossing and look both ways.”

Kabir rolled his eyes but came back to her side. They crossed safely with Grandma.

That night, after dinner, Meera sat down to play her favorite online game. A message popped up on the screen:
“Hi Meera! I saw your name on the leaderboard. Want to join my team?”
Meera didn’t recognize the name. She remembered her teacher’s rule: “Don’t chat with people online you don’t know in real life.”
She quickly clicked ‘Block and Report’ and told her dad.
Meera made three smart choices that day—and each one kept her safe.

Explore

What is Safety?
Safety means protecting yourself from danger or harm. It’s not about being afraid; it’s about being aware, alert, and ready. When we practice safety, we help keep our body, mind, and feelings safe too. Whether you are at home, in school, playing in the park, or exploring the internet, being safe means making good decisions that protect you and others around you.

Why Is Safety Important?

Safety is one of the most important life skills. It helps you:

- Avoid injuries or accidents.
- Build confidence in different situations.
- Think clearly during emergencies.
- Stay independent while being smart.

• Help others when they're in trouble.

By learning and practicing simple safety rules, you become stronger, wiser, and more responsible.

Where Do We Need to Stay Safe?

Let's look at some common places and situations where being safe really matters:

Place/Area	What to Watch Out For
Home	Fire, electrical wires, sharp objects, medicines
School	Slippery floors, staircases, bullying, rough play
Playgrounds	Unsafe swings, strangers, falling from height
Roads	Fast vehicles, traffic signals, zebra crossings
Online	Strangers, fake links, personal info sharing
Public Places	Getting lost, unfamiliar people, crowded areas

Safety is not just about big emergencies. It's about everyday actions that help you avoid trouble.

Try It: Create Your Safety Shield!

Materials: A blank sheet, crayons or sketch pens

Steps:
1. Draw a big shield in the center of your paper.
2. Divide it into 4 parts.
3. **Label them:** "Home," "School," "Outside," and "Online."
4. In each part, draw or write two things you do to stay safe in that area.

Example:

- **Home** – "I stay away from hot pots."
- **School** – "I walk, I don't run in the hallway."
- **Outside** – "I don't talk to strangers."
- **Online** – "I never share my photo with anyone."

Stick it in your room as your Safety Superhero Shield!

Think & Reflect

Let's pause and think:

1. Have you ever been in a situation where you had to make a quick decision to stay safe?
2. Who teaches you about safety—parents, teachers, friends, or someone else?
3. What do you think is the most important safety rule in your life right now?
4. Have you ever helped a friend or classmate stay safe? What happened?
5. Why do you think rules exist in schools, roads, and online platforms?

Write your answers in your notebook or talk about them in your next class discussion.

Let's Revise

Here's what we've learned in this chapter:

✔ Safety means protecting yourself from harm.
✔ It applies to many places—home, school, outdoors, online.
✔ Making safe choices is a sign of intelligence, not fear.
✔ Learning safety rules helps you feel strong, smart, and prepared.
✔ We all have the power to be safety heroes in our everyday life!

You don't need to be a grown-up to make safe choices—you just need to be smart and alert!

Check Yourself (Mini Assessment)

A. Multiple Choice Questions

What does safety mean?
a) Being scared
b) Staying away from people
c) Protecting yourself from harm ✔

What should you do if a stranger online asks for your address?
a) Tell them
b) Ignore it
c) Block and report ✔

Where should you cross the road?
a) In the middle of traffic
b) At the zebra crossing ✔
c) Near a parked car

Who is responsible for your safety?
a) Only your parents
b) Only your teachers
c) You, along with trusted adults ✔

B. True or False
1. You should always open the door if someone says they have a gift for you. ✗
2. Safety is only important when you're outside. ✗
3. Practicing safety helps you become more confident. ✔
4. Sharing your school name online is safe. ✗

C. Creative Task
Write a short paragraph about "One Time I Made a Safe Choice."

Explain what happened, what you did, and how it helped you or someone else.

Beyond the Book

Family Safety Challenge

Sit down with your family and make a list of 5 home safety rules. Stick the list on your refrigerator or your study wall.

Examples:

- Don't touch switches with wet hands.
- Keep medicines in the cabinet.
- Walk, don't run on stairs.
- Ask before using sharp tools.
- Know how to dial emergency numbers.

Also, practice a fire drill or "what to do during an emergency" at home. Make a plan—know where to exit and who to call.

Chapter 2

Staying Safe at Home

Story: The Curious Case of the Kitchen Alarm

Arjun was a smart and curious 11-year-old who loved helping his parents around the house. One Sunday morning, he decided to surprise his mom with toast and tea. He went into the kitchen, turned on the stove, and placed a metal pan on it. He couldn't find the mitts, so he used a towel to lift the kettle—and suddenly, the towel caught fire!

Panicking, Arjun waved it around. The flames grew.

Just then, his elder sister Priya entered. "Don't panic!" she shouted.

She grabbed a thick towel, covered the fire, and helped Arjun "stop, drop, and roll" to put out the burning cloth.

They turned off the stove, opened the windows, and called their parents.

Everyone was safe, but it could have been much worse.

That day, Arjun learned a powerful lesson: the home is a safe place only if we know how to stay safe.

Explore

Your home may feel like the safest place in the world—but there are hidden dangers in every corner. Fire, electricity, sharp tools, medicine, cleaning liquids—all of these can become risky if not handled properly.
Here's how you can stay safe in every room of your house:

Kitchen Safety

- Never cook alone unless an adult says it's okay.
- Stay away from hot stoves, pans, ovens, and toasters.
- Don't touch anything with wet hands, especially electrical switches or gas knobs.
- Don't wear loose clothes that can catch fire.

- **Learn "Stop, Drop, and Roll" in case of fire:**
  - o Stop running.
  - o Drop to the ground.
  - o Roll over to put out flames.

Electrical Safety
- Never put fingers or objects into electric sockets.
- Don't use appliances with wet hands or near water.
- Report broken wires or sparks to an adult immediately.
- Turn off switches before plugging/unplugging devices.

Sharp Objects Safety
- Don't play with knives, scissors, blades, or needles.
- Use stationery like scissors only with adult permission.
- Never try to cut fruits or vegetables alone.

Chemical & Cleaning Product Safety
Stay away from toilet cleaners, insect sprays, detergents, or acids.

Don't smell or touch liquids from unmarked bottles.
Never mix two cleaning liquids—it can create harmful fumes!

Medicine Safety

- Never take medicine on your own—even if you've had it before.
- Some medicines look like candy but can be dangerous.
- Keep medicines in a closed cupboard, away from young children.

Stranger Safety at Home

- Don't open the door to anyone you don't know—even if they say "I'm from the gas company" or "I have a gift for your parents."
- Use a peephole or window to check first.
- Call a trusted adult immediately if something feels off.

Toy & Furniture Safety

- Don't climb on chairs or shelves—you could fall.
- Keep the floor clean and toys picked up—so no one trips.
- Don't pull heavy objects that could fall on you.

Bathroom Safety

- Slippery floors can cause falls—walk slowly and carefully.
- Use a non-slip mat inside the shower or tub.
- Don't take very hot water—check the temperature first.

Try It: "Spot the Hazards" Activity

Instructions:

Look around your house. Use a notebook to make a list of:

- 3 safe things you see (e.g., plug covers, organized toys, dry floors)
- 3 unsafe things you see (e.g., wires on the floor, open medicine bottles, kitchen scissors lying out)

Now, talk to your parents about how to fix the unsafe items. You are now a Junior Safety Inspector at home!

Think & Reflect

1. Which room in your house do you think is the most dangerous? Why?
2. Have you ever helped prevent an accident at home? What did you do?
3. Who do you go to when you feel unsafe at home?
4. What is one habit you can start today to keep your home safer?

Write your answers in your safety journal or share them in class.

Let's Revise

Let's quickly remember the key takeaways:

✔ Never use fire, electricity, or sharp tools without adult help.
✔ Avoid wet hands near switches and appliances.
✔ Don't climb on furniture or play with cleaning items.
✔ Keep medicine away from reach and ask before taking any.
✔ Learn to say NO and alert an adult when a stranger knocks.

Your home is safe when you make safe choices every day.

Check Yourself (Mini Assessment)

A. Multiple Choice Questions

1. What should you do if your clothes catch fire?
a) Run fast
b) Pour water
c) Stop, drop, and roll ✔

2. What is a danger in the bathroom?
a) Bright lights
b) Wet floors ✔
c) Mirror

3. Which of these should not be touched?
a) Toothpaste
b) Plug socket ✔
c) Water bottle

4. What do you do if a stranger comes to the door?
a) Open the door
b) Look through peephole and call an adult ✔
c) Shout at them

B. True or False
You can touch plugs with wet hands if you are careful. ✗
Medicines are only to be taken with adult guidance. ✔
Mixing two cleaning liquids is safe. ✗
You should tell a parent if something smells strange in the kitchen. ✔

C. Creative Task
Draw a picture of your kitchen or living room.
Mark areas that are safe with ✔ and unsafe with ✗.

Then, write a few sentences about how you can make your home safer.

Beyond the Book

Family Safety Map Project
Make a Home Safety Map with your family.
1. Draw a floor plan of your home.

2. Mark:
- o Fire escape route
- o Emergency numbers
- o Safe meeting spot
- o First aid box location

3.Practice a quick fire drill or earthquake drill with your family. This small project can save lives in a real emergency!

Chapter 3

Safe Outside –

Parks, Roads & Public Places

Story: Kabir and the Kite Adventure

Kabir and his friends were excited. It was Sunday, and the community park was full of kites dancing in the sky. Kabir brought his new red kite and raced to the middle of the park, not noticing the cyclist zooming past. He stumbled—and nearly got hit!

Later, while chasing a runaway kite, Kabir followed it across the street. Thankfully, his friend Tara shouted, "Kabir, stop! Look for cars!" A speeding auto whizzed by—just where Kabir would have been.

That evening, a security guard found a child crying near the swing set. The boy had wandered away from his parents and didn't know what to do. Kabir and Tara helped him stay calm and asked the guard for help.

The park, the road, and public places are fun—but they also require smart thinking to stay safe.

Explore

Outdoor Fun, Outdoor Rules
Being outside is healthy and fun! We play, explore, walk, and learn new things. But it also means we're around vehicles, strangers, and open areas.

Staying safe outside means:
- Knowing your surroundings
- Paying attention
- Following rules
- Thinking before acting

Road Safety Rules

Roads can be dangerous if not used wisely.

Let's break down the golden rules for kids:
1. Use zebra crossings or pedestrian signals to cross the road.
2. Look left, right, and left again before crossing.
3. Hold an adult's hand if you're under 12.
4. Walk on the footpath, not the road.
5. Wear bright colors or reflectors when walking or cycling at night.
6. Never play on the road or chase balls into traffic.
7. Use foot overbridges or underpasses where available.

Fun Fact: In many countries, crossing the road at any random place is called "jaywalking"—and it's not just unsafe, it's illegal too!

Park Safety Rules

Parks are great for playing—but they can also be risky if you're not alert.
- Use age-appropriate swings, slides, and rides.
- Don't push or rush on the playground.

• Check if surfaces are hot or broken before using them.
• Be careful near ponds, fountains, or water bodies.
• Stay close to family or trusted adults.
• Don't accept food, toys, or balloons from strangers—even if they look friendly.
• If you get hurt or feel uncomfortable, speak up immediately.

Public Places Safety (Markets, Malls, Stations)

Public areas are often crowded. Getting lost or separated can be scary.
• Always stay within eyesight of your family.
• Memorize your full name, phone number, and address.
• If lost, stay in one place and ask a police officer, shopkeeper, or security guard for help.
• Don't run or hide—stay visible.
• Never leave the building or area to look for your family.

Tip: Parents can pin a small ID card in your pocket or bag with emergency contact details.

Stranger Safety Outside

Strangers are people you don't know. Not all strangers are bad—but it's important to be careful.
• Never go anywhere with someone you don't know—even if they say "Your mom sent me."
• Don't accept food, gifts, or rides from strangers.

• **If someone tries to grab you or makes you uncomfortable:**
  o Shout: "No! Leave me alone!"
  o Run to a safe place with people around.
  o Tell a trusted adult as soon as possible.

Learn Emergency Info

Every child should know:

- Their full name
- Parents' names
- Full home address
- At least one mobile number
- **Local police helpline:** 100 or 112
- **Child helpline (India):** 1098

Practice this with your family once a month!

Try It: "Safety Roleplay"

With your friends, act out these short safety situations:

1. You are trying to cross a busy road.
2. You are at a fair and lose sight of your parents.
3. A stranger offers you an ice cream.
4. You fall off the slide and hurt your knee.

Now, swap roles and act again. Afterward, talk about what you learned. This helps you prepare in a fun way!

Think & Reflect

1. Have you ever felt unsafe outside? What did you do?
2. Why do you think parks have age labels on rides?
3. Can strangers always be trusted if they wear a uniform?
4. Why is it important to remember your parents' phone number?
5. What would you do if your friend started running onto the road?

Write your thoughts or discuss them with a teacher or parent.

Let's Revise

Let's review the key takeaways:

✔ Roads must be crossed with care: use zebra crossings, not shortcuts.

✔ In parks, don't push or accept things from strangers.

✔ Stay near adults in crowded public places.

✔ Never leave with a stranger—even if they say it's urgent.

✔ Learn and practice your emergency information regularly.

Chapter 4

Online Safety –

Smart Kids, Safe Clicks

Story: The Mystery Message

Riya loved playing online games after finishing her homework. One evening, while playing a game on her tablet, a message popped up: "Hi Riya! I like your avatar. What's your real name? Let's meet sometime!"
Riya paused. She didn't know this person. The message seemed friendly, but something felt strange.

She remembered what her teacher had said:
"Online strangers are just like real-life strangers—sometimes dangerous."
So, Riya did the smart thing. She blocked the user, took a screenshot, and told her mom. Together, they reported the message and checked the privacy settings.

Riya felt proud—she had stayed safe online!

Explore

The Digital World Around Us
We use the internet to learn, play, watch, explore, and connect. It's an amazing place full of exciting things. But just like the real world, the digital world has rules, dangers, and safe zones.

Being safe online means:
• Thinking before you click
• Knowing what's okay to share
• Avoiding online strangers
• Protecting your personal information
• Reporting things that make you feel uncomfortable

Online Stranger Danger

Strangers online can pretend to be kids or say nice things to trick you. This is called online grooming and it can be very dangerous.

NEVER share:
• Your full name
• Address or phone number
• School name
• Daily routines (like where you play or go)
• Your photo or family pictures
• Passwords (not even with friends)

Remember: If someone online says, "Don't tell your parents," that's a red flag!

Online Content Safety

The internet has millions of videos, games, websites, and messages. Some are fun and helpful.
Others may be:

- Scary
- Violent
- Full of bad language
- Fake or misleading
- Unsafe for children

If you ever see something that makes you uncomfortable:

1. Close the page or app
2. Talk to a trusted adult
3. Don't forward or share it

Tip: Use "Safe Mode" or child filters when watching YouTube or browsing with parents.

Online Games & Chat Safety

Many games today allow you to:

- Chat with other players
- Join teams
- Trade items
- Share achievements

That sounds fun—but strangers may use chats to trick you.

Always:

- Use a nickname, not your real name
- Play with people you know
- Turn off public chat if possible
- Block and report bad behavior

Never:

- Share photos or videos
- Agree to meet someone offline
- Accept gifts or money from online players

Emails, Links & Downloads

You may receive emails or pop-ups saying:
• "You've won a prize!"
• "Click to claim your free game!"
• "Your computer has a virus—click here!"

These are mostly scams or malware. If you click, hackers can steal your information.

What to do?
• Never click suspicious links
• Don't open unknown emails or attachments
• Ask a parent before downloading anything
• Use antivirus software and secure browsers

Online Shopping & Money

Some websites or games ask for money to:
• Buy coins
• Unlock levels
• Get rewards or exclusive items
You should never buy anything online without asking your parents.

Using your parent's card without permission is also not safe and not right.

Social Media Smarts

Kids today love using apps like Instagram, WhatsApp, Snapchat, and YouTube. But these platforms are meant for older teens (usually 13+).
If you use them with family:
✔ Share only what's okay
✔ Keep profiles private

✔ Avoid talking to strangers
✔ Think before you post

Don't post:

- Your location or address
- School uniforms
- Personal problems
- Videos without permission

What goes online stays online forever!

Try It: Online Safety Checklist

Create a 2-column chart with headings:

- ✔ Safe Online Habits
- ✗ Unsafe Online Habits

Fill in at least 3 items in each column.

Examples:

✔ Safe Online Habits	✗ Unsafe Online Habits
Tell parents before clicking	Click random pop-up ads
Use strong passwords	Use same password everywhere
Block/report strangers	Talk privately to online strangers

Stick this near your computer or tablet as a daily reminder!

Think & Reflect

1. Have you ever seen something online that made you feel uncomfortable? What did you do?

2. Why is it dangerous to meet someone in person you only know

from a game or app?

3. Why should we ask before downloading apps or clicking links?

4. Can someone pretend to be your age online? What should you do?

5. How do you know a website or video is safe and child-friendly?

Let's Revise

Let's remember the important points:
✔ Don't share personal information online.
✔ Block and report strangers or bad messages.
✔ Never click suspicious links or emails.
✔ Don't download or shop online without permission.
✔ Think before you post on social media.

Being digitally smart keeps you safe and confident in the online world.

Check Yourself

A. Multiple Choice Questions
1. What should you do if someone online asks for your address?
a) Give it quickly
b) Ask a friend
c) Block and report ✔

2. What is a phishing email?
a) A funny video
b) A message that tricks you into clicking ✔
c) A game update

3. Why should you not share photos online?
a) They're boring
b) They use too much data
c) They can be misused ✔

4. Who can help you stay safe online?
a) Only the internet
b) Trusted adults ✔
c) Other online players

B. True or False
1. It's okay to give your school name online. ✗
2. Games with chat features can be risky. ✔
3. Social media is always safe. ✗
4. Bad websites should be reported. ✔

C. Creative Task

Design an Online Safety Superhero!
- Name them (e.g., CyberShield, NetSafe Nisha)
- Draw their costume and gadgets
- **Write a comic panel:** Show how they stop a stranger from tricking a child online

Share your drawing in class or with friends!

Beyond the Book

Family Digital Agreement
Sit down with your family and create a simple "Internet Use Agreement".

Include:
- Time limits
- No talking to strangers

- Asking before downloading
- Checking privacy settings
- Weekly “digital detox” time (no screen for 2 hours/day)

Write it, sign it, and put it near the computer/tablet!
Now your family is a Cyber-Safe Squad!

Chapter 5

Strangers, Tricks & Traps –

Learn to Say "No!"

Story: A Ride Too Risky

Aarav was waiting outside his school gate for his elder brother to pick him up. A man in a red car pulled up and rolled down the window.

"Hey there," the man smiled. "I'm your uncle's friend. He told me to take you home. Hop in!"

Aarav hesitated. The man seemed friendly. He even knew Aarav's name! But something didn't feel right.

Aarav took a step back, clutched his school bag, and ran inside the school office. "There's a stranger outside asking me to get in his car," he told the receptionist.

The stranger drove off quickly.

Later, it turned out no one had sent a car for Aarav. His alert thinking may have saved his life.

Explore

Who is a Stranger?

A stranger is anyone you do not know well or trust. They might look kind, friendly, or even wear a uniform. But if you've never met them with a trusted adult or don't know their name, they're a stranger. Not all strangers are dangerous, but you must never trust someone just because they smile or talk nicely.

Common Stranger Tricks

Strangers may use tricks to fool you. Here are some examples:

Trick Type	What They Might Say	What to Do
Gift Trick	"I have candy/toys for you. Just come with me!"	Say NO and walk away.
Fake Family Trick	"I'm your mom's friend. She told me to pick you up."	Ask for a password or run for help.
Lost Pet Trick	"Help me find my puppy near the trees."	Say NO. Do not follow them.
Emergency Trick	"Your dad is in the hospital. Come with me quickly!"	Confirm with an adult first.
Game/Photo Trick	"Let's take some fun pictures or play a secret game."	This is not okay—tell a trusted adult.

Stranger Safety Golden Rules

Do not go anywhere with someone you don't know—even if they offer help or gifts.

✔ Never share personal information, even your name or school.
✔ If someone makes you feel weird or scared, trust your instincts.
✔ Say NO loudly, run to a safe place, and tell an adult.
✔ Always inform your parents where you are, especially in public places.

Learn to Say "No!"

Saying "no" is not being rude—it is being safe and strong.

Practice saying:
- "No! I don't know you."
- "I don't talk to strangers."
- "You're not my parent—I'm not going with you."

Practice these lines with a teacher, friend, or family member using role play.

Understand Safe vs Unsafe Adults

Safe Adults are people you and your family trust. These include:
- Parents or guardians
- Teachers
- School principal
- Police officers in uniform
- Security guards (if known to your family)

Unsafe adults can be:
- Anyone who asks you to keep secrets from your parents
- Anyone who touches you inappropriately
- Anyone who tries to take you somewhere without permission

Secret Rule: If someone says "Don't tell your parents"—they are not safe.

Stranger Safety at School

• Never leave school with anyone unless your parent/teacher confirms it.
• If someone strange is waiting at the gate, inform your teacher.
• Always stay with a group while waiting.
• Know where the school office or security guard is.

Try It: Stranger Safety Roleplay

With a friend or sibling, act out the following situations:
1. Someone offers you candy near the school gate.
2. A man says he is a taxi driver and was sent to pick you up.
3. A woman tells you she lost her kitten and needs help.
4. A teen in the park asks you to come behind a tree for a "fun game."

After each act, pause and ask:
"What would you really do?"
Then, practice shouting: "NO! I need help!"

Think & Reflect

1. Why do you think some strangers use tricks to gain your trust?
2. What makes it hard to say "no" sometimes?
3. What do you feel in your body when something doesn't feel right?
4. Who are 3 trusted adults you can go to in an emergency?
Write your thoughts in a "Safety Journal" or talk to a grown-up about them.

Let's Revise

Let's review the key takeaways from this chapter:
✔ A stranger is someone you don't know or trust—even if they seem friendly.

✔ Some strangers use tricks to lure you—never fall for them.
✔ Learn to say NO loudly, run to safety, and tell a trusted adult.
✔ Safe adults are people your family knows and trusts.
✔ You have the right to feel safe, always.

Check Yourself

A. Multiple Choice Questions

1. What should you do if a stranger offers you candy?
a) Take it politely
b) Say no and walk away ✔
c) Ask for more

2. Who is a safe adult?
a) A random man at the park
b) A friend's uncle you've never met
c) Your school teacher ✔

3. If someone says "Don't tell your parents," you should:
a) Keep it a secret
b) Tell your parents immediately ✔
c) Think about it later

4. What is the best way to stay safe from strangers?
a) Trust your feelings ✔
b) Follow everyone
c) Take shortcuts

B. True or False
1. You must always help a stranger who says they lost their dog. ✗
2. It's okay to say NO to someone who makes you feel uncomfortable. ✔
3. If someone knows your name, they must be safe. ✗
4. Telling parents everything that happens is a good habit. ✔

C. Creative Task
Make a Stranger Safety Shield!

Draw a big shield. Divide it into 4 parts:
- A stranger trick you know
- Your safe adults
- What to say when you feel unsafe
- Places you can run to for help

Color it brightly and keep it in your school bag or room.

Beyond the Book

Family Code Word Challenge
Create a secret "Family Password" with your parents.
- If someone says they were sent by your parents, ask for the code word.
- If they don't know it—run away!

Practice using it once a month with fun role-plays.

Your code word could be something like:
"Blue Tiger" or "Pizza Rocket"
This small step can prevent a big danger.

Chapter 6

Emergency Ready! Fire, First Aid & More

Story: The Kitchen Spark

Nisha was making tea with her mother when suddenly, the cloth near the stove caught fire. Flames grew fast! Nisha froze for a second—but then remembered what she had learned at school: Stop, Drop, and Roll.

Her mom quickly turned off the gas and grabbed a wet towel to smother the flames. Nisha ran to get her younger brother and led him outside safely.

Later, her father said, "You were calm and smart. That's what saves lives during an emergency."

Emergencies can be scary, but if we are prepared and alert, we can keep ourselves and others safe.

Explore

What is an Emergency?

An emergency is a sudden, dangerous situation where quick action is needed to prevent harm or save lives.
Emergencies can happen anywhere—at home, school, outdoors, or even online.

Examples of emergencies:

- Fire
- Cuts or burns
- Earthquakes
- Fainting or choking
- Electric shock
- Getting lost

Being "emergency ready" means knowing:

- What to do
- Whom to call
- How to stay calm

Fire Safety

Common causes of fire:

- Kitchen gas stoves
- Electrical short circuits
- Candles or diyas left unattended
- Matchsticks or lighters used for fun
- Firecrackers

Do's during a fire:

✔ Shout and alert everyone
✔ Leave the area immediately
✔ Stay low if there's smoke
✔ Use stairs—not elevators

✔ Call 101 (fire emergency number)
✔ If clothes catch fire: STOP, DROP, and ROLL

Don’ts during a fire:
✗ Don’t hide in cupboards or under beds
✗ Don’t use water on oil fires
✗ Don’t go back inside for toys or things

First Aid Basics

First Aid is the help you give someone before a doctor arrives.

1. Cuts & Wounds
- Wash your hands
- Clean the wound with clean water
- Cover it with a bandage
- If there’s too much bleeding, press gently with a cloth

2. Burns
- Use cool (not cold) water
- Do not apply toothpaste or oil
- Cover lightly with a clean cloth
- Visit a doctor for serious burns

3. Nosebleeds
- Sit up and lean forward
- Pinch the soft part of the nose
- Breathe through the mouth
- Do not lie down or tilt head back

4. Fainting
- Help the person lie down
- Raise their legs a little
- Loosen tight clothes
- Call for help and ensure fresh air

Remember: First aid is not a replacement for medical care—it's the first step until help comes.

Electrical & Shock Safety

• Don't touch a person who is getting an electric shock—turn off the main switch first.
• Don't touch wet wires or broken plugs.
• If someone is shocked, call for help and don't panic.

Natural Disasters: Earthquake Safety

India is prone to earthquakes in some regions. Let's learn how to act smart.

During an earthquake:
✔ Drop, cover, and hold under a sturdy desk
✔ Stay away from windows or glass
✔ Don't run outside during shaking
✔ If outside, move to an open space
✔ After shaking stops, exit the building calmly

Emergency Numbers

Memorize or write down the following:

Emergency	Number
Fire	101
Police	100 or 112
Ambulance	108
Childline	1098
Disaster Helpline	1078

Post this list near your phone or study table.

Try It: Build a First Aid Box

At home, with an adult's help, collect the following in a small box:
Band-aids
Antiseptic liquid
Cotton and gauze
Small scissors
Hand sanitizer
Basic medicines (used with adult only)
Label the box: "Emergency First Aid – For Family Use Only"
Keep it in an easy-to-reach place, but away from young children.

Think & Reflect

1. Have you ever been in an emergency? **What did you do?**
2. Why is it important to stay calm during dangerous situations?
3. Who in your home knows basic first aid?
4. Can children help during emergencies? How?
5. What are some emergency drills you've done in school?

Discuss these questions with your classmates or write in your journal.

Let's Revise

Let's go over the key points:
✔ Emergencies can happen anytime—be alert and prepared
✔ Fire safety starts with stop, drop, and roll
✔ Learn basic first aid—clean wounds, treat burns, stop nosebleeds
✔ Know how to act during natural disasters like earthquakes
✔ Memorize emergency helpline numbers

Being ready helps you stay safe and help others too.

Check Yourself

A. Multiple Choice Questions

1. What number do you call for an ambulance?

a) 100
b) 108 ✔
c) 1098

2. What should you do if your clothes catch fire?

a) Run outside
b) Pour water
c) Stop, drop, and roll ✔

3. Which item should be in a first aid box?

a) Toys
b) Band-aids ✔
c) Spices

4. What should you do during an earthquake inside a classroom?

a) Hide under a desk ✔
b) Run outside
c) Stand near the window

B. True or False

1. First aid is the help you give after reaching the hospital. ✗
2. You should lie flat if you have a nosebleed. ✗
3. Call 101 for a fire emergency. ✔
4. It's safe to touch someone getting an electric shock. ✗

C. Creative Task

Make a poster titled "I Am Emergency Ready!"

Include drawings of:

- Fire escape steps
- Earthquake safety positions
- First aid box

• Emergency numbers

Write a simple slogan like:
"Stay Calm, Stay Smart, Stay Safe!"

Beyond the Book

Emergency Practice Drill

With your family, conduct a mock drill for these emergencies:
1. Fire in the kitchen
2. Earthquake while sleeping
3. Someone falls and gets a cut

Time each drill and discuss what went well and what can be improved.
Post your escape plan on the wall near your main door.
Now your family is Emergency Ready Heroes!

Chapter 7

Trust Your Gut –

Listening to Your Instincts

Story: An Uneasy Feeling

Sana was walking home from school when she noticed a man on a bicycle following her. He wasn't doing anything wrong—but he kept looking at her and slowed down when she turned.
Sana's heart started beating faster. She felt nervous. Her hands were sweaty. Her "gut feeling" was telling her: "Something's not right." So, she crossed to the other side of the road and walked into a nearby stationery shop where the shopkeeper knew her family. The man rode away. Later, her mom said, "Sana, you listened to your instincts. That's called being aware and brave."

Explore

What Are Instincts?
Instincts are those natural feelings inside us—our body's way of warning us when something feels "off" or unsafe. It's also called

your gut feeling, and it's one of your most powerful tools for safety. Sometimes, you may not be able to explain why something feels wrong-

but your body gives you signals:
• A tight stomach
• Sweaty hands
• Fast heartbeat
• Goosebumps
• Wanting to run away

These are signs that your instinct is alerting you. You must listen to it.

Trusting Your Feelings

It's okay to say:
• "I don't feel safe right now."
• "This place doesn't feel okay."
• "Something about this person makes me uncomfortable."

And it's always okay to:
• Say no
• Leave the place
• Tell a trusted adult

Even if the person seems nice or others say, "It's not a big deal."

Safe vs Unsafe Feelings

Let's learn to identify the difference:

Situation	Safe Feeling	Unsafe Feeling
Playing with trusted friends	Happy, relaxed, excited	-

Walking alone and someone follows	Nervous, cold, heartbeat rises	Uncomfortable, unsafe
Teacher explaining in class	Calm, focused, ready to learn	-
Someone touches you secretly	Confused, scared, want to hide	Uncomfortable, unsafe
Lost in a market	Anxious, scared, unsure	Unsafe, alert

Your feelings are your internal safety alarm. They help you know what's right and wrong.

Saying "No" Without Feeling Guilty

Sometimes children are told:

- "Don't be rude."
- "Just listen to elders."
- "Don't make a scene."

But your safety is more important than politeness.

If something or someone feels wrong, you can:

- Walk away
- Say "NO" loudly
- Ask for help
- Call a parent or teacher

And you never have to keep secrets that make you feel scared or confused.

Who Can You Talk To?

Your safety circle should include trusted adults you can go to when something feels wrong. **These can be:**

- Parents

• Siblings
• Teachers
• School counselor
• Neighbor you trust
• Grandparents

It's important to tell someone—even if you're not sure how to explain it.

The "Safety Box" Method

To help kids share what they're feeling, some schools use a Safety Box—a place where children can drop a note if something's bothering them.

At home, you can create a Safe Talk Diary where you write:
• What happened
• How you felt
• What you want to do

This helps you think clearly and speak up confidently.

Try It: Trust Your Gut Drama

With friends or classmates, act out the following scenes:
1. Someone asks you to go into a room alone.
2. A stranger follows you home from school.
3. A known person makes you feel uncomfortable.
4. A group of kids dares you to do something unsafe.

Ask: What did you feel? What would you do?
Then, practice saying:
"No, I don't feel safe."
"I need to go now."
"I'm telling a trusted adult."

Think & Reflect

1. Have you ever had a gut feeling that helped you avoid a problem?
2. What does your body feel like when you're nervous or unsafe?
3. Who do you trust enough to tell anything?
4. Why is it okay to walk away from something—even if others stay?
5. How can we help our friends when they feel unsafe?

Write your answers in a notebook or share during group time.

Let's Revise

Let's go over what we've learned:

✔ Instincts are your inner warning signals.
✔ Your body sends signs when something feels unsafe.
✔ It's okay to say NO and walk away—even from known people.
✔ You should always share your feelings with a trusted adult.
✔ You don't need to explain why—if it feels wrong, it is wrong.

Trust yourself. You are smarter than you think.

Check Yourself

A. Multiple Choice Questions

1. What is a "gut feeling"?

a) Hunger
b) A stomach illness
c) A warning feeling from inside ✔

2. What should you do if someone makes you feel unsafe?

a) Stay quiet
b) Tell a trusted adult ✔
c) Keep the secret

3. Which is a sign of feeling unsafe?

a) Laughing

b) Fast heartbeat ✔
c) Sleepiness

4. What's most important when you feel something's not right?
a) Be polite
b) Trust yourself ✔
c) Don't speak up

B. True or False
1. You must always listen to grown-ups—even if it feels wrong. ✗
2. Your body can tell you when danger is near. ✔
3. It's rude to say no to someone older than you. ✗
4. Keeping unsafe secrets is okay if you're scared. ✗

C. Creative Task

Design a **"Trust Yourself Badge"**
- Draw a circle
- Inside, write or draw things that help you feel safe
- Add your personal message like:

"My Feelings Matter"
"I Am Brave"
"I Will Speak Up"

Hang your badge on your school bag or study table!

Beyond the Book

Safety Circle Activity
Draw a big circle. Inside, write the names of 5 people you can trust if you feel scared or unsafe.

Label it:
"My Safe Adults"

Now ask those people, “Can I come to you if something bothers me?”

Stick this near your bed as a daily reminder.

You’ve built your Safety Circle—your first defense!

•

Chapter 8

Good Touch, Bad Touch –
Body Safety

Story: Asha's Secret

Asha was usually cheerful. But lately, she had stopped talking in class. She didn't want to play during lunch breaks. Her teacher, Ms. Reena, noticed something was wrong.

One day, Ms. Reena read a story to the class about "Good Touch and Bad Touch." After the session, Asha slowly walked up and whispered,

"Someone touched me in a way that made me feel scared… but they said not to tell anyone."
Ms. Reena knelt down and gently said, "You did the right thing, Asha. Thank you for telling me. I'm here to help you."

That day, Asha learned that her body is hers—and no one has the right to touch her in a way that makes her feel afraid or ashamed.

Explore

What is Body Safety?

Body safety means knowing:
• What kinds of touch are okay or not okay
• That your body belongs to YOU
• That you have the right to say NO
• That secrets that hurt you should never be kept
• That it's always okay to talk to a trusted adult

Every child has the right to feel safe and respected.

Good Touch vs. Bad Touch

Type of Touch	Examples	How It Makes You Feel
Good Touch	Hug from your parents, pat from teacher, holding hands to cross the road	Safe, loved, comfortable
Bad Touch	Touching your private parts, tickling that feels uncomfortable, forced kisses	Scared, sad, confused
Unwanted Touch	Even if someone says it's a game, but it feels "wrong"	Nervous, unsure, uncomfortable

Important Rule:
If any touch makes you feel confused, scared, or ashamed—it's not okay.

Understanding Private Parts

Teach children using the "swimsuit rule":

The parts of your body covered by a swimsuit are private. No one is allowed to:

- See them
- Touch them
- Ask you to touch theirs
- Show you pictures or videos of private parts

Even if someone says:

- "It's our secret."
- "You'll get into trouble if you tell."
- "It's just a game."

These are tricks. You must tell a trusted adult immediately.

Speak Up and Say "No!"

Saying "NO" is brave.

Practice saying:

- "No! I don't like that."
- "Stop it. I'll tell someone."
- "That's not okay!"

You can also:

- Run away from the situation
- Find a trusted adult
- Keep telling adults until someone listens

Even if the person is a relative, teacher, neighbor, or older child—you must speak up if they hurt you.

Who Are Trusted Adults?

Trusted adults are people who:
- Make you feel safe
- Listen when you talk
- Never keep secrets that hurt
- Take action to protect you

Examples:
- Parents
- Teachers
- School counselor
- Grandparents
- Family doctor
- Elder siblings

Secrets vs Surprises

Surprises are short-term and make people happy:
"Don't tell Dad about his birthday gift yet!"
Secrets about touch, pain, or fear are never okay.
"Don't tell anyone about what happened."
If someone asks you to keep a secret that makes you feel sad, scared, or unsafe—you must tell a trusted adult.

Try It: Roleplay – Safe or Unsafe?

With your classmates or family, act out these situations and decide:

1. Grandma gives you a goodnight hug.
2. A friend wants to look at your body in the toilet.
3. A cousin tells you, "Don't tell anyone about our special game."
4. A doctor examines you during check-up with your parent in the room.
5. A neighbor offers you sweets but also asks to sit on his lap.

After each one, answer:

Safe or Unsafe?
What should you do?

Think & Reflect

1. What makes you feel safe and respected?
2. Can someone you know and trust ever touch you in a bad way?
3. What would you do if someone touched you and told you to keep it a secret?
4. Do you find it hard to say NO? Why?
5. Who are 3 people you can talk to anytime about anything?

Write your answers in your "Body Safety Journal" or share in a group discussion.

Let's Revise

Let's remember the key messages:
✔ Your body belongs to you.
✔ Good touch makes you feel safe; bad touch makes you feel confused or afraid.
✔ Private parts are not for others to touch or see.
✔ It's okay to say NO loudly—even to known people.
✔ Always tell a trusted adult if you feel uncomfortable.
✔ Keep telling until someone listens.

You have the right to feel safe, heard, and protected.

Check Yourself

A. Multiple Choice Questions

1. What is the "swimsuit rule"?

a) Wear your swimsuit daily
b) Private parts are covered by swimsuits ✔
c) Don't play in water

2. What should you do if someone touches you in a way you don't like?
a) Stay quiet
b) Tell a trusted adult ✔
c) Keep it a secret

3. Who is a trusted adult?
a) A stranger on the road
b) A family member who makes you uncomfortable
c) Your teacher or parent ✔

4. Why is it okay to say "No" loudly?
a) To scare people
b) To be rude
c) To protect yourself ✔

B. True or False

1. It's okay to let someone touch your private parts during play. ✗
2. You should always keep secrets if someone tells you not to tell. ✗
3. You have the right to say "No." ✔
4. It's only bad if a stranger touches you in a wrong way.✗

C. Creative Task

Make a "Body Safety Promise Poster":
• **Write:** "I Promise to Protect Myself"
• Add 5 rules (e.g., Say NO, Speak up, Trust my feelings)
• Draw a badge or hand symbol
• Decorate it with stars or safe emojis
Put this up in your room or classroom!

Beyond the Book

Family Body Safety Talk

Have a gentle, open talk with your parents or guardian about:

- What is good touch and bad touch
- Who your trusted adults are
- How to respond if something feels wrong
- How to speak up without fear

Use body safety storybooks or videos to start the conversation.
Make your home a safe space where no question is too small.

Chapter 9

Being a Safety Hero for Others

Story: The Brave Bus Ride

Rohan was riding the school bus when he noticed something odd. A younger boy named Ishaan looked scared and was trying to move away from an older student who kept whispering to him and poking him. Rohan didn't stay silent. He told the bus monitor, who immediately moved Ishaan to the front seat and called the school counselor. Ishaan later told the counselor that he was being bullied daily. Thanks to Rohan's courage, Ishaan was safe—and Rohan became a safety hero.

Explore

Who is a Safety Hero?

A Safety Hero is someone who:

- Looks out for others
- Speaks up when they see something wrong

• Stands up against bullying or unsafe behavior
• Helps others stay calm during emergencies
• Shares what they've learned to protect others

You don't need to wear a cape to be a hero. You need awareness, kindness, and courage.

Spotting Unsafe Situations

Sometimes children feel something's wrong but don't know what to do.

Here are signs to watch for:
• A friend looks scared or wants to be alone often
• Someone always gets hurt during games
• A child cries after talking to an adult or older child
• Someone touches another person without their consent
• A kid is always being teased or laughed at
• A stranger is standing too close to children or offering gifts

Don't ignore these signs. If something doesn't feel right—it probably isn't.

The Bystander Effect

Many people see something unsafe happening but think:
• "Someone else will handle it."
• "I don't want to get involved."
• "What if I get in trouble?"

This is called the bystander effect—and it can stop people from helping. But you can choose to be different.

Be an upstander, not a bystander.

How to Help Safely

You can help without putting yourself in danger.

Situation	What You Can Do
Friend is bullied	Stay with them, speak up, report to a teacher
Someone is crying in the park	Ask if they're okay, take them to a trusted adult
A classmate looks scared	Sit with them, ask questions gently, tell an adult
You see someone being touched	Interrupt the situation, distract, report immediately
In an emergency (fire, fall)	Call for help, don't panic, support others until help comes

You are not responsible for solving everything—but you can be the bridge to help.

When to Tell a Trusted Adult

Some kids worry that telling an adult is "snitching" or "tattling." Here's the rule:
If someone is hurt, scared, or in danger, you must tell.
It's not tattling. It's caring.

Trusted adults you can report to:

- Teachers
- Parents
- Principal
- School counselor
- Bus monitor
- Security guard

Creating a Safety Culture

Being a Safety Hero also means:

- Including others in play
- Respecting others' boundaries
- Speaking kindly
- Helping new students feel welcome
- Teaching younger kids about safety rules

A safe classroom or playground is where everyone feels seen and heard.

Try It: Safety Hero Roleplay

Act out these scenes in groups:

1. A friend is being teased for their lunchbox.
2. You see a younger student looking scared near the gate.
3. During a field trip, someone wanders away.
4. A classmate tells you a teacher hit them.

Discuss:

- What would you do?
- Who would you tell?
- How would you stay calm?

Then, create your "Hero Statement" and say it out loud:
"I will speak up. I will help. I will keep others safe."

Think & Reflect

1. Have you ever seen someone being treated unfairly or unsafely?
2. Did you help or stay quiet? Why?
3. What scares you about helping others?
4. Who do you feel most safe talking to?
5. How can you help a friend who's afraid to speak up?

Write your answers or discuss in your group journal.

Let's Revise

Let's remember the key messages:

✔ A Safety Hero watches out for others

✔ You must speak up if you see something wrong

✔ Helping doesn't mean solving—it means reporting and supporting

✔ Never be afraid to tell a trusted adult

✔ Creating a safety culture starts with YOU

Your voice can protect someone else.

Check Yourself

A. Multiple Choice Questions

1. What should you do if you see someone being bullied?

a) Laugh along

b) Walk away

c) Stay with the person and tell a teacher ✔

2. What does "bystander effect" mean?

a) Helping always

b) Hoping others will act instead of you ✔

c) Wearing a cape

3. Who is a trusted adult?

a) Random neighbor

b) Teacher or school counselor ✔

c) Online gamer

4. What is NOT part of being a safety hero?

a) Helping others

b) Keeping unsafe secrets ✔

c) Creating a safe environment

B. True or False

1. Speaking up for others is being dramatic. ✗
2. You can be a safety hero by telling an adult. ✔
3. It's wrong to help someone being hurt. ✗
4. Everyone can make others feel safer. ✔

C. Creative Task

Design your own Safety Hero Card

Include:

- Your Hero Name
- Your Safety Powers (Listening, Reporting, Including, Encouraging)
- A Hero Motto (e.g., "Speak Up, Help Out!")
- A symbol or badge (shield, star, lightbulb)

Hang it on your wall or keep it in your school bag.

Beyond the Book

Build a **"Safety Buddy Club"**

At school or in your group:

1. Create a group of students who check in on others.
2. Meet weekly to share ideas for making your school safer.
3. Post kind notes, lead safety games, or mentor younger kids.
4. Take turns being the "Safety Captain of the Week."

Celebrate being a Kindness Hero and a Safety Star!

Chapter 10

My Safety Pledge and Everyday Habits

Story: The Safety Champion

Every Friday at school, the class voted for a "Weekly Champion." One week, the award went to Avni—not for scoring highest in maths or winning a race, but for something different.
That week,

She:

- Helped a friend say NO when someone touched her uncomfortably
- Spoke up when she saw loose wires in the science lab
- Wore her helmet every day on the bike to school
- Reminded classmates to use the zebra crossing on a field trip

Avni was chosen because she practiced everyday safety habits—and helped others do the same.
Her teacher called her "Our Safety Star."
And Avni? She just smiled and said, "It's what we all should do."

Explore

What is a Safety Pledge?
A Safety Pledge is a promise you make to yourself to stay aware, responsible, and alert every day. It's like a secret agreement between you and your inner Safety Hero.

It reminds you to:
- Make safe choices
- Use your voice to say no
- Watch out for others
- Keep learning about safety

Taking a pledge doesn't mean you'll never make mistakes—but it means you care about doing what's right.

Everyday Safety Habits

Here are safety habits that smart children follow every day:
At Home
- Never touch electrical switches or wires with wet hands
- Stay away from fire, gas stoves, and sharp objects
- Ask before using medicine
- Keep the bathroom dry to avoid slipping
- Lock doors properly at night

Outside
- Use footpaths and zebra crossings
- Hold an adult's hand near traffic
- Don't talk to or follow strangers
- Stay in well-lit places
- Carry emergency contact details

Online
- Don't share personal info or passwords

- Report strangers or bad content
- Use devices in visible spaces
- Think before clicking or sharing
- Don't download without permission

Body & Feelings
- Say "No" to bad touch or confusing games
- Trust your gut instincts
- Talk to your safety circle if something feels wrong
- Speak up for others
- Never keep secrets that hurt

Morning Safety Checklist

Start your day by checking:
✔ Did I lock my school bag properly?
✔ Am I carrying my ID card or parent contact info?
✔ Did I wear proper shoes?
✔ Do I have a snack and water?
✔ Am I wearing a helmet (if cycling)?
✔ Do I feel ready and aware?

Just 1 minute every morning helps keep your day safe!

The "Three Ask Rule"

If something bad happens or feels wrong:
1. Ask for help from an adult
2. If no one listens, ask someone else
3. If still not helped, ask again until someone takes action

Never stop asking until you feel safe again.

My Safety Pledge

Stand tall, take a deep breath, and repeat:

I am strong.
I am smart.
I stay safe and help others stay safe.
I listen to my instincts.
I say NO when something feels wrong.
I don't keep unsafe secrets.
I tell trusted adults and ask for help.
I will be a Safety Hero, every day.

Now write it down, decorate it, and hang it in your room!

Try It: Create Your Safety Diary

In a small notebook, write:

- One safety habit you practiced today
- One thing that made you feel proud
- One new safety fact you learned

Write in it every night for one week.

At the end, ask yourself:
"Did I grow as a Safety Hero?"

Think & Reflect

1. Which safety habits are easy for you?
2. Which ones are still hard to remember?
3. Who helps you stay safe every day?
4. What will you do if someone near you forgets a safety rule?
5. How can you encourage your friends to follow safety habits?

Let's Revise

Let's review what we've learned:

✔ A Safety Pledge is your personal promise to stay safe
✔ Good habits start with small, daily actions

✔ Being consistent builds confidence
✔ You can help make safety fun and normal for others
✔ You are never too small to make a big difference
Every step, every choice, every word—matters!

Check Yourself

A. Multiple Choice Questions

1. What is a Safety Pledge?
a) A game
b) A promise to follow safety habits ✔
c) A list of punishments

2. What should you do if your friend forgets to wear a helmet?
a) Laugh at them
b) Remind them kindly ✔
c) Ignore it

3. How often should you talk to trusted adults if something feels wrong?
a) Once
b) Keep asking until someone helps ✔
c) Never

4. What's a good morning safety habit?
a) Skipping breakfast
b) Locking your bag ✔
c) Forgetting your ID

B. True or False
1. A safety hero only helps themselves. ✗
2. You should talk about unsafe secrets. ✔
3. Wearing a helmet is a safety habit. ✔
4. Children can't help others stay safe. ✗

C. Creative Task
Design a “My Daily Safety Shield”

Draw a big shield and divide it into 4 parts:
1. One home safety habit
2. One outdoor safety habit
3. One online safety habit
4. One way I help others

Color it, decorate it, and share it with your class!

Beyond the Book

Make a Family Safety Calendar

With your parents:
• Pick one safety habit per day for a week
• Write it on a calendar
• Practice it together (like turning off switches, crossing safely)
• Put gold stars when completed!

At the end of the week, hold a “Family Safety Star” ceremony and give each other fun titles like:
• “Helmet Hero”
• “Kitchen Guardian”
• “Emergency Expert”

Celebrate safety, together!

Summary

Stay Safe, Stay Smart – Your Safety Handbook is a comprehensive, child-friendly guide designed for students in Grades 3–8 to understand personal safety in all areas of life. Aligned with NEP 2020 and NCF 2023, this book empowers children with the knowledge, skills, and confidence to protect themselves in everyday and emergency situations.

The book covers safety at home, in public places, on the internet, in emergencies, and in interactions with strangers. It teaches the difference between good touch and bad touch, encourages speaking up, and promotes the idea that children can be safety heroes not just for themselves but for others too.

Using stories, checklists, reflection questions, and activities, the book helps children develop safe habits, strong instincts, and a caring mindset. Each chapter follows an engaging format focused on critical thinking, experiential learning, and 21st-century life skills.

Safety is not just a rule – it's a way of life.

Every child deserves to feel safe, and this handbook makes that possible through joyful and meaningful learning.

Glossary of Safety Terms

Term	Meaning
Emergency	A sudden situation needing quick action to stay safe
Instinct	A natural feeling that something is right or wrong
Trusted Adult	A grown-up you know well and feel safe talking to

First Aid	The first help given before a doctor arrives
Bad Touch	Any touch that makes you feel scared, uncomfortable, or confused
Safety Circle	A group of people you trust and can go to for help
Bystander Effect	When people don't help because they think someone else will
Stranger Danger	The idea that unknown people can sometimes be unsafe
Online Grooming	When someone tries to trick or manipulate you through the internet
Body Safety	Knowing your rights and rules to keep your body and feelings safe

Check Yourself – Answer Key

Chapter 1–10 quiz answers (summarized):

- **Chapter 1:** 1–c, 2–c, 3–b
- **Chapter 2:** 1–c, 2–b, 3–b, 4–b
- **Chapter 3:** 1–c, 2–b, 3–c, 4–c
- **Chapter 4:** 1–c, 2–b, 3–c, 4–b
- **Chapter 5:** 1–b, 2–c, 3–b, 4–a
- **Chapter 6:** 1–b, 2–c, 3–b, 4–a
- **Chapter 7:** 1–c, 2–b, 3–b, 4–b
- **Chapter 8:** 1–b, 2–b, 3–c, 4–c

• **Chapter 9:** 1–c, 2–b, 3–b, 4–b

• **Chapter 10:** 1–b, 2–b, 3–b, 4–b

Beyond the Book – Real-Life Safety Projects

Here are fun and practical ideas to extend learning beyond the pages!

1. Safety Map of My Neighborhood

Make a large drawing of your neighborhood:
• Mark your house, school, shops, parks
• Show safe routes, zebra crossings, and danger zones
• Add safety signs and labels

Present it during school safety week!

2. Create a Safety Song or Rap

Write a catchy 4-line song or rap using safety keywords:
• Road, helmet, fire, safe, online, no, stranger
• Perform it during assembly or record a short video!

Example:
"Look left, look right, cross with care,
Say NO to strangers anywhere!"

3. Build a DIY First Aid Kit

With adult help, collect first-aid items and label each one:
• Band-aid, gauze, antiseptic, thermometer
• Add usage notes or emoji stickers
• Practice using it (with guidance)

4. Body Safety Comic Strip

Draw a 4-frame comic showing:

- A bad touch situation
- How the child feels
- How they speak up
- How a trusted adult helps

Share it with friends and family to raise awareness.

5. Family Safety Week Challenge

Each day, do one task together:

- Practice a fire drill
- Review emergency contacts
- Walk the safest route to school
- Check electricity and gas safety
- Make a Safety Pledge together

Award “Safety Stars” to each family member!